The
MAGNIFICENT
MAKERS
The Great Germ Hunt

Go on more
a-MAZE-ing adventures with

The MAGNIFICENT MAKERS

The MAGNIFICENT MAKERS 4

The Great Germ Hunt

by Theanne Griffith
illustrated by Reggie Brown

A STEPPING STONE BOOK™
Random House 🏠 New York

Text copyright © 2021 by Theanne Griffith
Cover art and interior illustrations copyright © 2021 by Reginald Brown

Visit us on the Web!
rhcbooks.com

Educators and librarians, for a variety of teaching tools, visit us at
RHTeachersLibrarians.com

Library of Congress Cataloging-in-Publication Data
Names: Griffith, Theanne, author. | Brown, Reggie, illustrator.
Title: The great germ hunt / by Theanne Griffith ;
illustrated by Reggie Brown.
Description: First edition. | New York : Random House Children's Books, [2021] |
Series: The magnificent makers ; 4 | "A Stepping Stone book." |
Summary: In the Maker Maze, third graders Violet and Pablo, along with their classmate Aria, learn about good and bad germs and why it is important to stay home until fully recovered from an illness.
Identifiers: LCCN 2020044612 (print) | LCCN 2020044613 (ebook) |
ISBN 978-0-593-37960-8 (trade pbk.) | ISBN 978-0-593-37961-5 (library binding) |
ISBN 978-0-593-37962-2 (ebook)
Subjects: CYAC: Viruses—Fiction. | Sick—Fiction. | Makerspaces—Fiction.
Classification: LCC PZ7.1.G7527 Gr 2021 (print) | LCC PZ7.1.G7527 (ebook) |
DDC [Fic]—dc23

Printed in the United States of America
10 9 8 7 6 5 4 3 2 1

First Edition

This book has been officially leveled by using
the F&P Text Level Gradient™ Leveling System.

Thanks for all those library visits, Daddy.
−T.G.

To my wonderful nephews,
Nino and Gino, who love to read
−R.B.

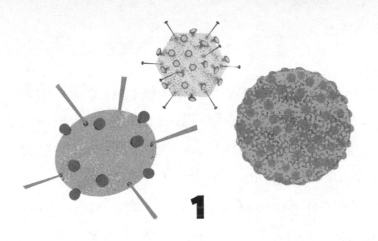

"*Achooooooo!*" Violet sneezed.

"Bless you!" Pablo eyed his best friend. "Do you need . . . a tissue?" he asked.

"No, thanks. I've got one," Violet replied. She opened her backpack and removed a small packet of tissues. She blew her nose.

"Are you sure you're feeling better?" asked Pablo. Violet was finally back at school after being home with a really bad cold last week.

"Definitely! My fever's gone. My body

doesn't ache anymore. I've been feeling great since yesterday! But my dad wanted to keep me home an extra day. Just in case." Violet cleared her throat. "It's probably my allergies." She blew her nose again. Loudly. "You know I always get them in the fall."

"Yeah, that's true," Pablo agreed.

Mr. Eng's third-grade students waited patiently for the day to begin. Violet was so happy to be in class again. Being home sick wasn't fun. Even though her parents let her have *a lot* more screen time than normal, she was lonely and missed school. And she really missed Pablo.

Pablo missed Violet, too. They were best friends, after all! They usually did just about everything together. They played soccer during recess. They sat next to each other during lunch and ate their favorite food: pickles! And every day they walked home together. But while Violet was sick, Pablo had to do all those things alone.

"Mira!" Pablo stretched his neck as he looked over Violet's shoulder. He pointed with his nose toward the round tables in the Science Space at the back of the classroom. The Science Space was filled with cool equipment. It had everything from magnifying glasses and magnets to drones and telescopes. Today, each table had its very own microscope sitting in the middle!

Violet's eyes grew wide with excitement. She rubbed her hands together. "This is exactly what I'm going to be doing when I grow up. Looking at squirmy germs under a microscope," she said with a smile.

Both Violet and Pablo loved science. Pablo's favorite was learning about planets and faraway galaxies. He hoped to travel to space one day in his very own space-ship. Violet was fine staying on Earth. She wanted to run her own laboratory and become famous for curing different types of diseases—especially colds.

"*Achooooooo!*" Violet sneezed again.

"Bless you!" said Mr. Eng. He walked over to their desks with a cage in one of his hands. "You *are* feeling better, right, Violet?" he asked.

Violet sniffled. "Yup! It's just my allergies."

"Well, I'm glad to hear that," said Mr. Eng. "I get allergies this time of year, too. I want to introduce you to our new class pet. Meet Max the mouse." He held the cage in front of Violet and Pablo for them to see.

Squeak!

"I think he just said *hi!*" Pablo giggled.

"Awww! He's so cute!" said Violet. "But . . . when do we get to use the microscopes, Mr. Eng?"

"Very soon." He winked.

"I can't wait! Today is going to be amazing!" said Violet.

As Mr. Eng walked Max to the next set of desks, Pablo whispered, "I bet today is going to be *a-MAZE-ing.*"

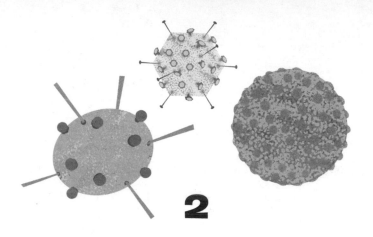

2

*D*ing! *Ding! Ding!*

Mr. Eng rang the bell on his desk. The students settled down. But a hum of excitement still vibrated throughout the classroom.

"Okay, class," he began. "We're starting a new unit this week. We'll be learning about different kinds of germs."

Aria, a student sitting near Pablo and Violet, shivered in her seat.

"I don't like germs," Aria said.

Mr. Eng smiled. "Some germs are icky

and can make us sick. But did you know there are a lot of good germs, too?"

Before Violet could agree, she let out another loud sneeze. *"Achooooooo!"*

"Bless you!" said Pablo.

Mr. Eng squinted his eyes and paused before picking up a pile of worksheets from his desk. "Today we're going to learn about three types of germs: bacteria, viruses, and fungi."

Pablo raised his hand. "Fung-what?"

"FUN-guy," Mr. Eng repeated slowly. "Let's head over to the Science Space and get started." He pointed to the back of the classroom with his pencil. "Please sit in groups of three."

"This is the most beautiful microscope ever!" said Violet as she took her seat at one of the round tables.

"Yeah, and it's red!" added Pablo. Red was their favorite color.

"Can Aria join your group?" Mr. Eng asked. "She is a little unsure about germs. Maybe you can help her out?"

"Sure!" said Violet and Pablo together.

Aria slowly took a seat next to Pablo. She watched Violet rub her nose with her sleeve.

"You sure you're not sick?" Aria asked.

Violet smiled. "Oh, I'm fine. My nose just itches. My allergies always bother me in the fall," she said, looking outside. The trees were covered with orange and red leaves. Then Violet read the handout:

NAME: _____

Getting Germy

Bacteria are everywhere. Even on your skin! They're made up of just one cell. Some cause infections, but some types of bacteria are good for us!

Viruses need to be inside another living thing to grow. Viruses are very, very small. The flu is caused by a virus.

Most fungi are made up of many cells. They get their nutrients from other living things. When they grow on us, they can cause rashes. But many are harmless!

Mr. Eng waved his pencil in the air. "Okay, class. Let's go over the handout."

Violet knew she should be paying attention. This was stuff she needed to know to run her disease-destroying laboratory. But the microscope was just too cool! She couldn't resist. Violet leaned over the table and took a peek.

No way, she thought.

Violet tapped Pablo on the shoulder. "It's a riddle!" she whispered.

"Where?" he asked.

"In the microscope!" Violet replied.

Pablo leaned over to have a look.

"What's going on?" asked Aria quietly.

But Pablo didn't hear her. "Whoa! You're right!" he said.

He read the tiny riddle in a hushed voice:

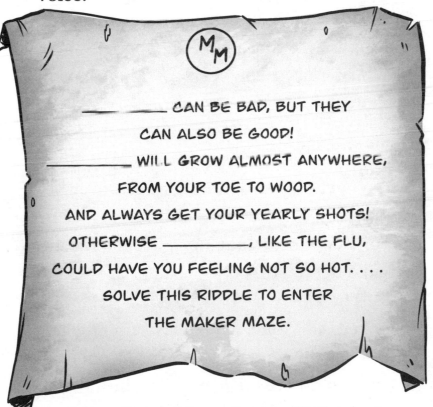

_____ CAN BE BAD, BUT THEY
CAN ALSO BE GOOD!
_____ WILL GROW ALMOST ANYWHERE,
FROM YOUR TOE TO WOOD.
AND ALWAYS GET YOUR YEARLY SHOTS!
OTHERWISE _____, LIKE THE FLU,
COULD HAVE YOU FEELING NOT SO HOT. . . .
SOLVE THIS RIDDLE TO ENTER
THE MAKER MAZE.

Aria adjusted her glasses. "What's the Maker Maze?" she asked.

"Imagine the Science Space," Pablo replied. Then he smiled. "But a *million* times more awesome."

"A *trillion* times!" whispered Violet. "If we solve this, we get to go there. *And* go on a super-amazing science challenge."

Aria raised one eyebrow. She was still confused.

"You'll see," said Pablo. "At least, I think so. . . ."

Violet bit her lip and glanced over her shoulder. Mr. Eng was still talking. "The worksheet said that not all bacteria are bad. I bet the first one is bacteria."

"The flu is a virus," added Aria. She looked at Violet, who was rubbing her nose again with her sleeve. "Hopefully you don't still have it . . . ," she mumbled.

Violet quickly lowered her hand and

crossed her arms. "I had a cold, not the flu," she replied.

"Does that mean a fungus can grow on your toe?" Pablo interrupted. "Yuck!"

Without warning, the ground began to shake. The round tables trembled. The shiny red microscope wobbled and nearly fell over.

Aria gripped her seat. "What did we do?" she asked. Her glasses bounced along her nose.

Violet smiled. "We just opened a portal."

BOOM! SNAP! WHIZ! ZAP!

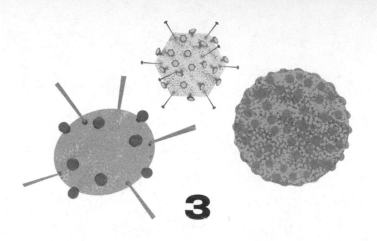

3

The shaking stopped. Everything was still. And everyone was frozen! Except for Violet, Pablo, and Aria. Aria's glasses swung from one of her ears. Her mouth hung open.

"What just happened?" she asked.

"I told you," replied Violet. "We opened a portal. That's how we get to the Maker Maze."

Aria fixed her glasses and closed her mouth. "Is that it?" She pointed toward

the table near Mr.
Eng. Next to Max's cage
was a rack of tubes. They were glowing
inside a circle of fuzzy purple light.

Violet, Pablo, and Aria tiptoed over.

"How are we going to fit through
there?" asked Aria.

Violet leaned in for a look.

BIZZAP!

Before she could answer, Violet was
shrunk down to the size of a pea and
sucked through one of the tubes!

"Where did she go?" Aria squeaked.

"I'll show you," said Pablo with a smile. He took her hand and leaned forward.

BIZZAP!

They both shrunk and were squeezed through the purple portal.

Pablo and Aria landed butt-first on the floor of the Maker Maze.

"Achooooo!" Violet greeted them with a sneeze. "What took you guys so long?" she joked.

"Bless you . . . ," Aria said slowly. Her eyes sparkled as she stood up and dusted herself off. "You weren't kidding. This is amazing! I've never seen anything like it before. What is this stuff?"

The room was filled with all types of science equipment. Colorful liquids bubbled inside flasks on a lab table. Across from the flasks were rows of different kinds of plants. One of them had flower buds that looked like eyeballs! Nearby, crystals floated in clear boxes, and bugs buzzed around in jars. Next to a long hallway lined with doors was a giant microscope.

"Welcome to the Maker Maze!" said Violet with open arms.

All of a sudden, the trio heard a soft hum coming from the long hallway. It sounded far away. But it was getting closer and closer. And louder and louder . . .

"What is that?" asked Aria with a shaky voice.

Suddenly, a voice shouted, "GET OUT OF THE WAY!"

Heading toward them at full speed was a robot! It blasted down the hallway on a single wheel with its arms and claws stretched up over its round head. The Makers jumped to the side just in time.

POW!

The robot crashed into a wall and exploded. All that remained was a pile of metal on the floor. A small stream of smoke floated toward the ceiling. Dr. Crisp blew into the room. Her rainbow hair was even more wild than usual.

"Is . . . everyone . . . okay?" she asked, trying to catch her breath.

"We're okay, Dr. Crisp. That was a close one!" Violet replied.

Dr. Crisp dusted off her lab coat and purple pants. She straightened her name tag. "My apologies. I was making some repairs, and, well—"

"Who are you?" Aria interrupted.

"I'm Dr. Crisp! I run this place. Nice to meet you, Aria."

"You know my name. . . ." Aria smiled.

"I sure do! Glad you decided to join Violet and Pablo today!" Dr. Crisp walked over to a lab table and picked up a glittery golden book. "So, Makers, what's the adventure of the day?" Dr. Crisp opened to a page with a large question mark on it.

"Cool! What's that?" Aria asked.

"It's the Maker Manual!" Pablo replied. "We decide what we want to learn, and the Maze creates a challenge for us."

Violet grabbed Aria's arm and held it up. "And we use our Magnificent Maker Watches to keep track of time! We only have one hundred twenty Maker Minutes to finish."

Aria smiled at the watch that had appeared on her wrist. But then she pulled her arm away. "You haven't washed your hands since the last time you sneezed on them."

Violet blushed. "Sorry," she mumbled. Then she turned to Dr. Crisp. "If we ask to learn about germs, will we get to use a microscope?"

Before Dr. Crisp could reply, the pages

of the Maker Manual started turning. They turned faster and faster until stopping on a page that read:

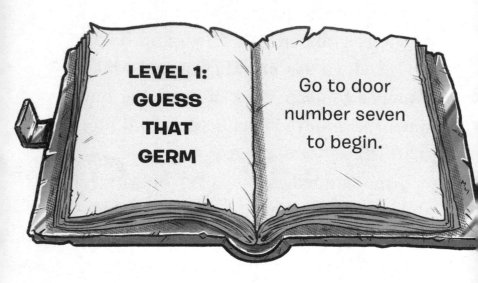

LEVEL 1: GUESS THAT GERM

Go to door number seven to begin.

"I think that was a Maker Maze *yes*." Dr. Crisp winked.

"Yay!" cheered Pablo and Violet.

Aria hesitated. "I want to learn about germs. But I don't want to catch any."

"Don't worry," said Pablo. "Nothing

can hurt you in the Maker Maze." He put his three middle fingers down in the shape of an *M*. "Maker's honor."

Aria took a deep breath and pushed her glasses up her nose. "Okay." She smiled.

Dr. Crisp grabbed a backpack from the floor and flung the golden book inside. She strapped it to her back and cart-wheeled down the never-ending hallway.

"We're going to have a *magnificent* time!" her voice echoed.

The Makers hurried behind.

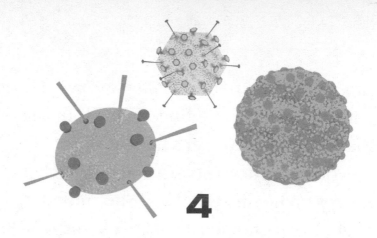

4

"This has got to be the best day of my life!" Violet exclaimed as soon as she walked through door number seven.

A long lab table was in the middle of the room. In the center of the table was a huge purple microscope! It had robotic arms coming out of the sides.

"Awesome!" said Aria.

"Allow me to present Morgan the Marvelous Microscope!" said Dr. Crisp, skipping toward the table. The Makers eagerly followed.

"Listen up!" Dr. Crisp began. "In this level, you're going to use this beauty to take a close look at some germs. Morgan is an extra-special scope. You'll be able to see the smallest of small things. Like viruses!" Dr. Crisp pulled a magnifying glass out of her lab coat pocket and held it up to her eye, which looked enormous behind the glass.

Violet, Pablo, and Aria laughed. But Violet's laugh turned into a sneeze. *"Achooooooo!"*

"Piping pipettes!" Dr. Crisp leaned closer to inspect Violet. The magnifying glass was still in front of her eye. "You're not sick, are you?" she asked.

"She was sick all last week," said Aria as she inched away from Violet.

"But I'm not anymore!" Violet said quickly. "I get allergies every fall," she explained.

"Glad to hear it. I need to stay healthy!" said Dr. Crisp with her hand on her chest. "Too much work here in the Maker Maze!"

"And *we* have a lot of work to do, too," Pablo said,

tapping his Magnificent Maker Watch. Then he turned to Aria. "If we don't finish in time, we don't get to come back to the Maker Maze."

Dr. Crisp continued. "You're going to use Morgan to identify bacteria, viruses, and fungi."

"Gross," said Aria. She rubbed her hands along her arms. "I don't want to get those germs on me."

"Never fear, our personal protective equipment is here!" replied Dr. Crisp. She opened her backpack and pulled out three pairs of lab gloves and safety goggles, and three white lab coats. "Time to put on your PPE!"

Aria adjusted her glasses. "How did that all fit in there?" she asked.

"Oh wow! We finally get to wear our own lab coats!" said Violet.

"I feel like a real scientist now!" Pablo put on his PPE.

"Good! Because you *are* a real scientist." Dr. Crisp winked. Then she pressed a button on the side of her watch and yelled, "Maker Maze, activate Morgan the Marvelous Microscope!"

BOOM! SNAP! WHIZ! ZAP!

A blast of purple light flashed from the giant scope. The robotic arms zipped into action and grabbed a small piece of glass from the table. It was strange to see something so small between such big robot claws.

"What is that?" asked Pablo. He scratched his cheek.

"It's a slide!" replied Violet.

"A slide?" Aria repeated.

"Not like the ones on playgrounds." Violet giggled.

"Correct!" said Dr. Crisp. She and Violet tapped elbows. "You shouldn't try to put your tush on these! To look at something with a microscope, we have to put it on a *slide* first."

"I've been waiting for this day for, like . . . *forever*!" said Violet, doing a happy dance.

"We are going to look at three slides," Dr. Crisp said, holding up three fingers. Then she pointed three fingers at the Makers. "And you'll have to guess what's on each." Dr. Crisp pressed a button on her watch. A purple light blasted out. A list appeared in the air.

Bacteria
Viruses
Fungi

"Ready, set, GUESS!"

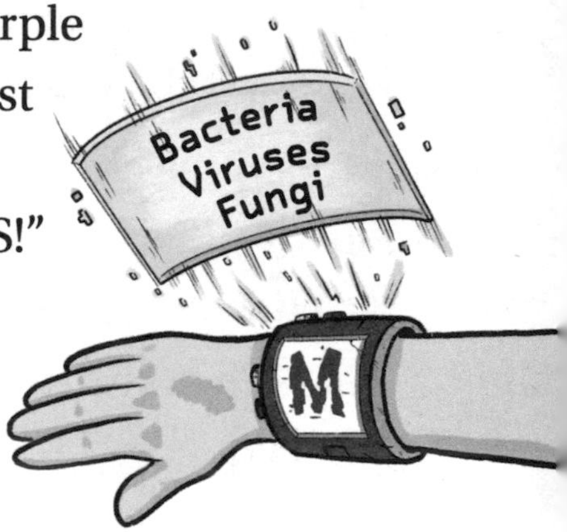

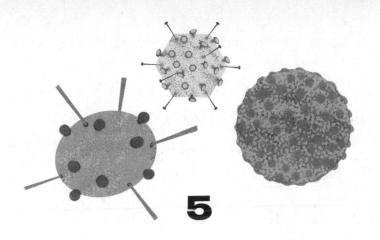

5

"**C**an I go first?" asked Violet.

Pablo and Aria said, "Sure!"

Violet was tall, but she couldn't quite reach the eyepiece on the massive microscope. Dr. Crisp spotted a step stool in the corner. She ran over and slid along the floor to grab it like a baseball player stealing second base. Then she pitched it across the room. Pablo grabbed his cheeks and closed his eyes. . . . But the stool landed perfectly next to Violet.

She smiled. "Thanks!" She hopped up.

Violet looked through the microscope and saw a bunch of little rod-shaped critters jiggling away on the slide.

"It's a germ party!" Violet laughed. "This is so cool!"

Aria shivered.

"Can I have a look?" asked Pablo.

Violet nodded. Then something started to tickle her throat. She tried to hold it down, but a loud cough escaped.

"Flaming flasks!" said Dr. Crisp. "That doesn't sound good!"

"Just got a little spit down the wrong tube," Violet said with her voice crackling.

"Sounds like germs are having a party in your throat," said Aria with a scrunched-up face.

Pablo giggled. But Violet didn't think it was so funny.

"I just got excited!" Violet replied more clearly. She began tapping her foot. "And I already told you, I get allergies in the fall."

"Come on. Let's not waste time," said Pablo, pointing to his watch. He took Violet's place on the step stool.

"Whoa," he said. "They're almost like little pills."

Finally, Aria hopped up to have a look. She wiped the eyepiece off with her lab coat. She wanted to make sure there was nothing left of Violet's cough on it.

"This is cool," she said. "But also gross." She adjusted her glasses and quickly hopped down. Just as her feet hit the floor, the robotic arms of the microscope snapped back into action. They put a new slide in place.

Violet got into position on the stool. She bit her lip. "I wonder what this is. It looks beautiful and nasty at the same time." She laughed as she stepped down.

Pablo climbed up. "It kind of looks like a dandelion."

"Maybe a mutant dandelion," replied

Violet. She glanced at Aria out of the side of her eye. "Your turn."

Aria gulped and stepped onto the stool.

"*Eeeeeeew!*" she said. "I don't want to be anywhere near that." She scurried back down.

"Don't worry!" said Dr. Crisp. She snapped the end of her glove and karate kicked an imaginary germ in the air. "PPE keeps the germs off me!" She winked. "And you, too!"

Aria looked at the ground. "It's just . . . ," she said, bringing her shoulders to her ears. But before she could finish, the robotic arms began twisting and moving as they put the final slide in place.

"Never mind. I just don't like to get sick," Aria finished.

"Yeah, it's not fun," said Violet. Then her nose started to wiggle. *"Achooooo!"* She sneezed into her elbow.

Before Aria could complain, Violet hopped back up onto the stool.

"Wow, these are super small. I can barely see them!" She squinted. "And they have little spikes or something coming out of them."

Pablo took a turn. "They look like little aliens! Maybe they're space germs!" he said.

When it was Aria's turn, she said, "I bet they're viruses. They're so much smaller than the others. And the handout said viruses were super tiny."

RING! DING! DONG!

The Maker Maze jingle sounded.

"Awesome, Aria! You got it right!" said Pablo.

"Love seeing those Maker minds at work!" cheered Dr. Crisp.

"Now we just have to figure out the other two slides," said Violet.

"I bet slide two was some kind of fungus. It looked like it was made up of a lot of cells. Not just one," said Pablo.

"Yeah!" added Violet. "And the germs on the first slide looked like single cells. But they were a lot bigger than the viruses. They must be bacteria!"

RING! DING! DONG!

"Well, flip my funnel! You folks are

good at this!" said Dr. Crisp. She tapped elbows with each of the Makers. Everyone removed their PPE. Dr. Crisp stuffed it all into her backpack.

"That was a lot of fun!" said Aria. "Gross. But fun!"

"What's next?" asked Violet and Pablo.

"Let's find out!" Dr. Crisp removed the Maker Manual from her backpack. It snapped open. The pages flipped until landing on one that read:

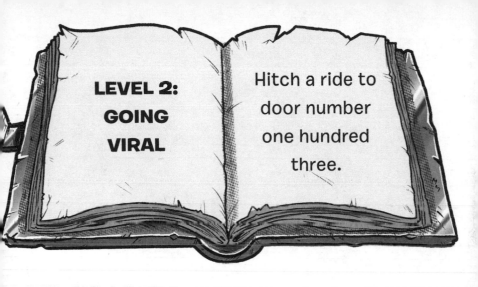

LEVEL 2: GOING VIRAL

Hitch a ride to door number one hundred three.

"One hundred three!" Violet couldn't believe it.

"How are we going to get there?" asked Pablo. He held his watch in the air. "That's going to take forever!"

Dr. Crisp smiled, then shouted into her watch, "Maker Maze, activate rapid robots!"

BOOM! SNAP! WHIZ! ZAP!

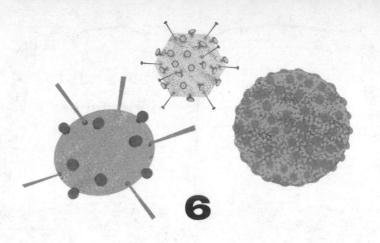

6

The ground began to shake. Out of nowhere, a hidden door in the floor opened. A circular platform rose, holding four shiny robots. Each one sat on a single wheel and had a round face with two eyes that glowed.

Aria raised her eyebrows. "That looks like the one that crashed earlier," she said.

"That robot went a little . . ." Dr. Crisp paused and scratched her head with her pencil. "Off the rails!" she finished. "These are working just fine. Hop on, Makers!"

She grabbed her backpack and jumped on a stand attached to the back of the robot.

Violet ran over and jumped on hers. Pablo followed, but Aria stayed behind. "Promise it won't crash?" Aria asked.

Dr. Crisp made the Maker's honor sign and said, "Promise!"

Pablo looked at his watch. It read *ninety-five minutes.* About an hour and a half left. "We should get going," he said.

Aria straightened her shoulders and said, "Okay. Let's do this."

Dr. Crisp pressed a button on her watch. A purple laser shot out! She aimed it at the wall in front of them. Suddenly, a hidden door opened.

The Makers' jaws dropped. "Cool!" they said.

Then Dr. Crisp yelled, "Hold on tight!" She pointed to two hooks in the robots' shoulders.

Without warning, the robots launched forward at full speed. They zoomed out of the room and turned sharply down the

never-ending hallway. The Makers held on tightly. They were going so fast their hair formed Mohawks.

"Yippeeeeee!" Dr. Crisp hollered. She pulled a lasso from her lab coat and whipped it overhead.

Violet laughed and tilted her head back. "Woo-hoo!" she yelled.

The robots came to a screeching halt at door number one hundred three.

The Makers jumped off. "Can we ride again?" Violet asked with a wide, toothy smile.

"Soon enough!" Dr. Crisp winked. She tossed her rainbow hair over her shoulder. "But for now, follow me!"

The Makers shook themselves out and hurried through the open door.

The room was large and empty.

"Okay, Makers!" Dr. Crisp said, tapping her watch. "It's that time!"

Aria adjusted her glasses and asked, "What time?"

Violet and Pablo jumped in the air and replied, "Making time!"

"Oh, I love making!" Then Aria pointed down at her left leg. "My mom and I 3D printed this," she said.

"Whoa!" said Pablo.

"That's so cool!" added Violet.

Dr. Crisp pulled out the Maker Manual. It snapped open to a page with three circular shapes at the top.

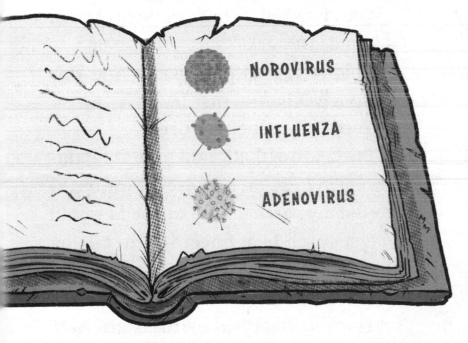

"*In-flu-EN-zuh?*" asked Aria, looking closely. "Like the flu?"

"Yes indeedy!" replied Dr. Crisp.

"What about this one?" asked Violet.

"Ah-deh-no-VI-rus." Dr. Crisp sounded out the strange name. "These viruses give you . . . *colds,*" she said slowly with raised eyebrows.

Violet blushed. "That's the virus I must have had last week!"

Pablo scratched his cheek. "And this one? Is it *NOR-uh-vi-rus*?"

"Yuppers!" replied Dr. Crisp.

"I've heard of that!" said Aria. "My family wanted to go on a cruise for my birthday. But my parents were worried I would get a stomach bug. I heard them talking one night about this virus. I'm pretty sure they called it norovirus!"

"That's correct! Noroviruses are *NOT* tummy-friendly," said Dr. Crisp, rubbing hers. Then she opened her backpack and began tossing supplies over her shoulder.

Tubs of different color clay and bags holding all kinds of pins flew through the air. They landed on the ground in front of the Makers. "For the first part of level two, you are going to build model viruses!" She pointed to the list of instructions in the Maker Manual. Then, through cupped hands, she shouted, "Ready, set, BUILD!"

Violet bit her lip. "We should make each virus a different color," she said, pointing to the tubs of purple, blue, and white clay.

"Sounds good," said Pablo. They each grabbed a tub and rolled the clay into balls.

Violet held hers in her hands. "The Maker Manual says this is the *capsid*."

"It's like the virus's body," said Pablo, reading over the instructions.

"Now, time to add these," said Aria. She held the bags of pins up by her ears. Some were long and pointy, and others were short with round-button tops. One bag had pins with colorful six-sided flat heads.

"It says here that those are viral proteins. They help the virus get into cells." Pablo continued reading.

"Looks like I'll need some of the long pins and the round ones for the influenza virus," said Violet.

"I need a few of those long ones, too," said Pablo, holding the model adenovirus. "And the flat ones with the hexagon heads."

Aria handed out the pins. She took some of the round ones. "The norovirus doesn't have any of those pointy ones. Just a bunch of these small button-shaped ones."

The Makers stuck the viral protein pins into the capsids.

RING! DING! DONG!

"Gasping goggles! Those viruses look *STEM-tacular*!" Then Dr. Crisp shouted into her watch. "Maker Maze, GO VIRAL!"

BOOM! SNAP! WHIZ! ZAP!

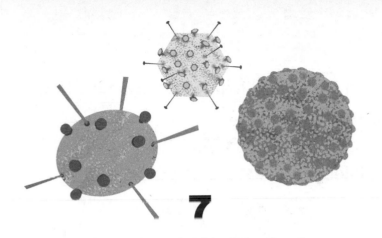

7

The room went dark. As the light returned, three holograms appeared.

"Whoa!" said Aria. She couldn't believe what she was seeing. She adjusted her glasses.

"Is that . . . me?" she asked.

"They're holograms!" Violet replied.

The holograms seemed to be at a summer camp. Hologram Violet was sitting at a picnic table eating a big slice of pickle pizza. Across from Violet, Hologram Pablo and Hologram Aria were playing a board game.

"Hey!" said Pablo. "How come only Violet gets to eat pickle pizza?"

"I wouldn't get jealous yet, space cadet!" replied Dr. Crisp. "When I say *three,* I want you to throw your viruses as high as you can into the air."

The Makers exchanged confused looks.

"And then I want you to press that button." Dr. Crisp pointed to their Magnificent Maker Watches. "Ready?"

Dr. Crisp skipped *one* and *two* and simply shouted, "THREE!"

Violet, Pablo, and Aria launched the model viruses into the air and activated their watches.

BIZZAP!

Three lasers shot out from the Makers' wrists and zapped the viruses, which disappeared.

"Awesome!" cheered Aria.

"Where did they go?" asked Pablo.

Dr. Crisp put her hand over her eyes as if she was searching for them. "They're still here." She paused. "Somewhere . . ."

Aria's eyes darted around the room. She crossed her arms and hugged her shoulders.

Then Dr. Crisp smiled. "Don't worry. They can't harm us." She walked toward the holograms. "But *they* might start feeling under the weather soon. By now, one of those viruses has made their way to each of your holograms." She spun around. Her lab coat twirled behind her. "You Makers will have to figure out which virus infected which hologram."

Violet tilted her head as she looked at Aria. "Are you okay?"

Aria didn't respond. She seemed frozen in place. Little sweat drops started to form on her forehead. Finally, in a shaky voice, Aria replied, "I don't know."

Just then, Violet let out three loud sneezes in a row.

"Achooooo! Achooooo! Achooooo!"

"Bless you!" said Dr. Crisp. "You feeling okay, Violet?"

"Yes, I'm fine." Violet cleared her throat. "Same thing happens to me every fall. It's so annoying."

"What could you be allergic to here in the Maker Maze?" asked Aria with her hands out at her sides.

"I'm fine! We need to focus on finishing this level." Violet turned to the holograms.

"I suppose you're right," said Pablo. "This one is going to be hard."

Dr. Crisp whipped a construction hat out of her backpack. It had a lightbulb sticking out of the top. "You'll definitely need your thinking caps!"

The Makers giggled.

Then Dr. Crisp said, "Ready, set, OBSERVE!"

∿

Violet, Pablo, and Aria watched the holograms closely.

"Nothing's happening," said Aria.

Suddenly, Hologram Violet stopped eating her pizza. She set it down and grabbed her stomach.

"Uh-oh," said Pablo. "Hologram Violet looks like she's going to barf!"

"Gross. You're going to make *me* barf," said Aria, holding her own stomach.

Then Hologram Aria started coughing. And then sneezing! She rubbed her throat. And kept coughing!

"Looks like your hologram is coming down with the flu!" said Violet. She put her hand to her ear and waited to hear the

Maker Maze jingle. But the room was still silent.

"Humph," Violet said with a frown.

"Nothing's happening to my hologram," said Pablo.

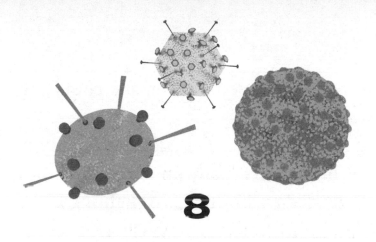

8

"I can't get sick." Aria was finally able to spit out the words. She lifted her arm slowly and pointed toward her hologram. "It's really, really not good."

"Oh, don't worry," Violet began.

But Aria interrupted. "I have to worry. If I get a bad cold, I don't stay at home for a week." She turned and looked Violet straight in the eyes. "I go to the hospital for a week."

Violet tried to search for the right

words. But the only thing she could say was "Why?"

Aria let out a low sigh and replied, "Well, we don't really know. It has something to do with my germ-fighting cells. They have a harder time getting rid of bacteria and viruses that get inside me," Aria explained. "The doctors say I'm *medically fragile.*" Then she adjusted her glasses and stood tall. "But I don't think I'm fragile. I think I'm tough."

"Stronger than steel!" said Dr. Crisp, flexing both of her arms.

Aria laughed. But her laughter was interrupted by a loud sneeze from Violet.

"Achooooo!"

Aria's eyebrows crinkled, and she frowned. "That's why it's important to stay home if you're still sick."

"But, Aria, I promise!" Violet insisted.

"I felt *sooooooo* much better. I was fine yesterday. I just get like this in the fall. It's the trees or something."

"Violet wouldn't lie." Pablo put his hand on his best friend's shoulder.

"But there aren't any trees here!" Aria said.

Squeak!

The Makers grew silent. Dr. Crisp's ears lifted as she listened closely.

"What was that?" asked Aria.

"I haven't the slightest clue . . . ," replied Dr. Crisp.

Squeak!

"There it is again!" said Pablo.

"Look!" said Violet. She pointed to Dr. Crisp's lab coat.

Peeking out of the front pocket was the new class pet, Max the mouse!

Dr. Crisp looked down and yelped, "Jumping Jupiter!" Her cheeks turned redder than the red stripe in her hair. "How did he . . . ummm . . . errr . . . ?"

"Maybe he snuck out of

his cage and followed us through the—" began Violet. *"Achoooo!"*

"Violet!" said Pablo. "That's it! It's Max!"

"Max?" she repeated.

"Maybe you're allergic to Max," Pablo continued. "That would explain why you started sneezing once you got back to school!"

Violet's eyes widened as she bit her lip. "I think you're right. I'm definitely allergic to my cousin's pet gerbil!"

"Maybe you're allergic to rodents?" Aria suggested softly.

Violet tilted her head back and moaned. "I feel like I'm allergic to everything!"

Aria looked down at her feet. "I'm sorry I made you feel bad for sneezing and coughing. I really thought you were still sick."

Violet smiled. "It's okay!" she replied. "I get why you would be nervous. But I'm glad you know I was being responsible. I would never want to get anyone sick."

Dr. Crisp quickly pulled a small cage for Max out of her backpack. "We can keep mischievous Max safe here for the rest of the challenge." She held it up and said, "This cage is anti-allergy!"

"Like my aunt's hairless cat!" said Aria.

Everyone laughed.

Then suddenly, Pablo cried, "Oh no! We only have thirty-five Maker Minutes left!"

"It's okay. We can do this!" said Violet. "Back to the challenge."

The Makers huddled.

"Hologram Aria doesn't have the flu. You already guessed that, Violet," said Pablo.

"And Hologram Pablo doesn't seem sick at all," added Aria.

Violet bit her lip. "That's it!" she said suddenly. "Every year, we get flu shots."

"Yeah! It even said so in the riddle!" said Pablo.

"Maybe the flu virus *did* go into Hologram Pablo. But the vaccine prevented him from getting sick?" Violet said.

(((((*RING! DING! DONG!*)))))

"Holy cow-culators!" shouted Dr. Crisp. "Very impressive!"

"Hologram Violet probably has the norovirus, since that makes your stomach ache," said Aria.

RING! DING! DONG!

"Which means the adenovirus gave Hologram Aria a cold!" replied Violet.

RING! DING! DONG!

"Fee-fi-fo-fum!" Dr. Crisp stomped across the room. "That's how Magnificent Makers get it done!" She tossed her construction hat into the air. "Great teamwork!"

Violet pushed a stray kink of hair out of her face. "That was hard!"

"Well, dust yourselves off, Makers! We still have one more level to complete!"

Dr. Crisp grabbed the Maker Manual. It snapped open. The pages turned in a flurry until suddenly stopping.

LEVEL 3: COUGH IT UP

Stay where you are.

Dr. Crisp jumped up and down and clapped her hands. "Oh, this is a fun one!" Then she shouted into her watch: "Maker Maze, activate Incredible Incubator!"

BOOM! SNAP! WHIZ! ZAP!

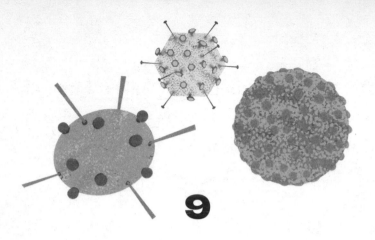

9

The holograms vanished in a flash of purple light. In the center of the room, a large square machine with knobs and buttons appeared. Next to it was a lab table lined with small, round plastic containers.

"What's that?" asked Aria, pointing to the machine.

Dr. Crisp walked toward it and set Max on the lab table. "This is the Maker Maze's very own turbo-powered, high-speed incubator!" she replied.

"What's an incubator?" asked Pablo, scratching his cheek.

"An incubator is a machine we scientists often use in experiments. It keeps the environment just right so we can grow cool stuff!" Dr. Crisp explained.

"Like germs!" added Violet.

"Bingo!" said Dr. Crisp, giving a thumbs-up. "Speaking of germs, time to put on our PPE!"

Dr. Crisp began to explain the last level as she pulled the Makers' gear from her backpack. "We are about to grow some germs. YOUR germs!" Dr. Crisp picked up one of the round containers. "On these! This is a petri dish." It was filled with something that looked like clear, firm Jell-O.

"*PEE-tree* dish," Violet, Pablo, and Aria repeated slowly.

"What's that stuff inside?" asked Violet.

Dr. Crisp removed the lid. "It's called agar. That's a fancy name for germ food."

AGAR

"AH-gur," said Aria. "Yuck!" She stuck out her tongue.

Dr. Crisp turned away from the Makers. "Stand back!" she said. She took a deep breath and coughed onto the petri dish and agar. Then she opened the incubator and slid the container inside. She quickly closed the door and pressed the big green *start* button. The Incredible Incubator began shaking and making strange beeping sounds. Max's anti-allergy cage rattled on the table along with the other petri dishes.

Squeak!

"What's happening?" asked Pablo.

"It's going to explode!" said Aria.

"Nope! It's just working some Maker Maze magic!" Dr. Crisp shouted over the noise of the incubator. "Normally, growing germs takes many hours. But thanks to our Incredible Incubator, in a few seconds you'll be in for a surprise!"

DING!

Dr. Crisp smiled and opened the machine. A little steam came out as she removed the dish. When she turned around and showed it to Violet, Pablo, and Aria, they couldn't believe what they saw.

Violet's eyes grew wide with amazement. "Are those germs?" she asked. The agar was covered with tiny little dots. There were hundreds of them!

"You bet your beaker they are! *My* germs!" replied Dr. Crisp.

holding a clean one in the air, "you *don't* want to send any germs onto it."

"Huh?" said Pablo, scratching his cheek.

"So . . . we have to cough on it," began Violet, "but not spread germs?"

"You got it, lab boss!" replied Dr. Crisp. "Not a single germ can be on the dish when you take it out of the Incredible Incubator."

"How are we going to do that?" asked Aria.

"That's what we have to figure out," replied Pablo. He looked at his watch. "And we only have twenty Maker Minutes left!"

"To keep things safe," Dr. Crisp continued, "only one of you will

"And we're going to get to grow our germs?" asked Violet, bouncing in p. She couldn't keep her excitement ins

"Well," said Dr. Crisp, "there's a tw

"There's always a twist," Pablo s Aria with a smile.

"For this level, you'll need to onto these petri dishes. But," sh

be doing the coughing. The other two will stand behind this line." She pressed a button on her watch.

BIZZAP!

A laser shot out. Dr. Crisp used it to mark the floor on the opposite side of the room.

"Can I be the cougher?" asked Aria. "It actually looks . . . fun."

"Go ahead!" said Violet and Pablo.

Aria smiled and ran over to the Incredible Incubator. She picked up a petri dish.

Then Dr. Crisp shouted, "Ready, set, COUGH IT UP!"

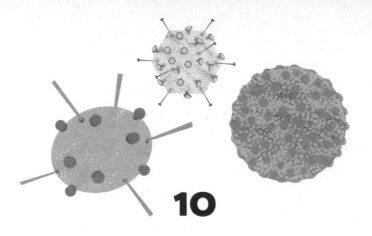

10

"**W**hat if you cover your mouth?" Violet shouted to Aria.

"Okay!" Aria held the petri dish in front of her face and coughed through her gloved hand. Then she covered the dish and placed it in the incubator and pressed *start.*

DING!

"There's definitely not as many germs," shouted Aria, holding the petri dish up for Violet and Pablo to see. "But there are still plenty there."

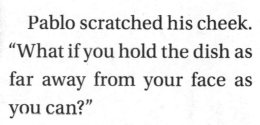

Pablo scratched his cheek. "What if you hold the dish as far away from your face as you can?"

"Like this?" said Aria. She grabbed a new dish and held it in her outstretched hand.

"Yeah! Give it a try!" cheered Violet.

Aria let out another cough and put this dish in the incubator.

DING!

"Nope!" Aria yelled. "That definitely didn't work. There's even more germs than before!"

"We've got to figure this out soon!" said Pablo, looking at his Magnificent Maker Watch.

Violet bit her lip. "I have an idea! What if you cover

your mouth with your hand AND hold the petri dish far away?"

"Got it!" Aria shouted back. She tried Violet's suggestion. But when she took the dish out of the Incredible Incubator, it still had a few germs on it.

The Makers were stumped. And they only had ten Maker Minutes left!

Then, suddenly, Pablo said, "Wait a minute!" He looked down at his gloved hands and lab coat. He raised his hands and gripped his goggles. "We use PPE to keep the germs off us," he began.

Violet nodded and listened carefully.

"What if we used PPE to stop *spreading* germs, too?" Pablo finished.

"Yes!" cheered Violet. "We need something to cover Aria's mouth."

Pablo paused. "Maybe a mask?" he suggested.

"Perfect!" Violet and Pablo tapped elbows. Violet shouted over to Dr. Crisp. "Do you have any masks, Dr. Crisp?"

"I thought you'd never ask!" Dr. Crisp dug in her backpack and pulled out a

purple mask. She jumped in the air and flung it like a slingshot over to Aria.

Aria leaped up and grabbed it. She fixed it to her face and coughed onto the petri dish. Aria quickly opened the Incredible Incubator and plopped the dish inside. Then she waited. And waited.

Suddenly, Dr. Crisp's watch flashed purple.

"We only have three more minutes!" Pablo shouted.

DING!

Aria held her breath and opened the incubator door. She

removed the plate and examined it. Then she turned around to face her friends.

"Did it work?" asked Violet.

Aria held the dish high in the air and pulled off her mask. "Yes!" she said as she jumped. "No germs!"

"We did it! We figured it out!" said Violet. "Masks must be really helpful for stopping the spread of germs!"

RING! DING! DONG!

"PPE is how we stay germ-free!" said Dr. Crisp. "But we don't have much time to celebrate! We're at door number one hundred three, and the portal closes in two minutes!" Then she shouted into her watch, "Maker Maze, activate rapid robots."

BOOM! SNAP! WHIZ! ZAP!

The room began to shake. A door in the ceiling opened, and a ramp lowered. Four robots rolled down.

"Hurry, Makers! Take off your PPE and hop on!"

Violet, Pablo, and Aria tossed aside their goggles, gloves, and lab coats. Aria grabbed Max off the lab table.

As soon as everyone was in position, the robots zoomed out of the room and down the never-ending hallway. The Makers were going so fast that the wind blew tears out of their eyes.

Squeeeeeak! Max cried from his cage.

"We're not going to make it!" Pablo hollered.

Finally, they arrived at the main lab.

Dr. Crisp hopped off her robot. Her pants snagged on one of the robot's claws.

"Hurry! It's closing!" Dr. Crisp pointed to the portal on the ceiling.

"Come on!" Violet yelled.

The Makers huddled together.

"Ready?" said Pablo. "JUMP!"

They squatted and pressed into the ground as hard as they could and jumped.

BOOM! SNAP! WHIZ! ZAP!

They shot out of the tiny test tubes and landed on the floor of the Science Space.

"Hurry! Our classmates are still frozen!" said Pablo.

"Achooooo!" Violet sneezed.

"Uh-oh, anti-allergy cage is gone!" said Aria. She was still on the floor. Max was perched in her lap.

"Quick, put him back!" said Pablo, pointing to Max's Science Space cage.

Just as they made it to their seats, everyone else unfroze.

"Okay, class," said Mr. Eng. "Who's

ready to use our microscopes? We're going to look at bacteria from different kinds of yogurt." He started passing out a test tube to each table.

Violet bit her lip. "Does Mr. Eng have a rip in his pants?" she asked.

"I think so . . . ," whispered Aria as she adjusted her glasses.

Mr. Eng walked up to their group. "Just the moment you've been waiting for, right, Violet?" He smiled.

"Yup! So glad we made it back in . . . ," she began. But Pablo nudged her knee under the table.

Mr. Eng raised his eyebrows and waited for her to finish.

"Um . . . I mean . . . pass the slides, please!"

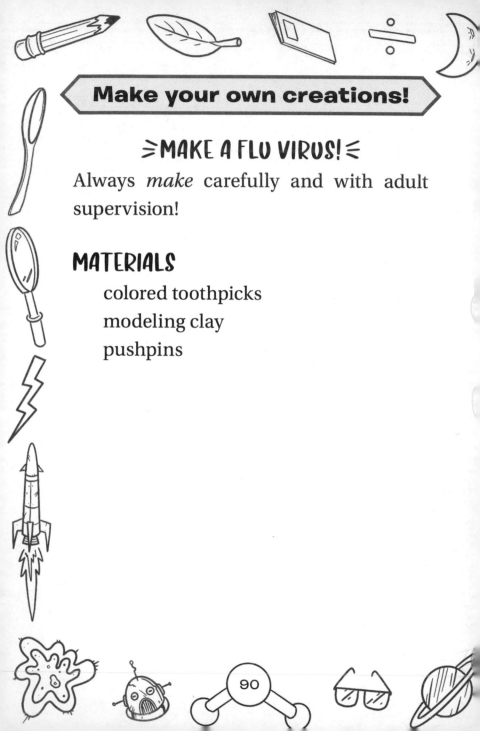

Make your own creations!

≥MAKE A FLU VIRUS!≤

Always *make* carefully and with adult supervision!

MATERIALS

- colored toothpicks
- modeling clay
- pushpins

INSTRUCTIONS

1. Mold your modeling clay into a ball. This is the virus's body, also called a capsid!

2. Stick a mix of pushpins and tooth-picks into the clay. These are the viral proteins that help viruses get into cells!

3. Experiment with different clay colors and different arrangements of pins to make other kinds of viruses, like adenoviruses and noroviruses!

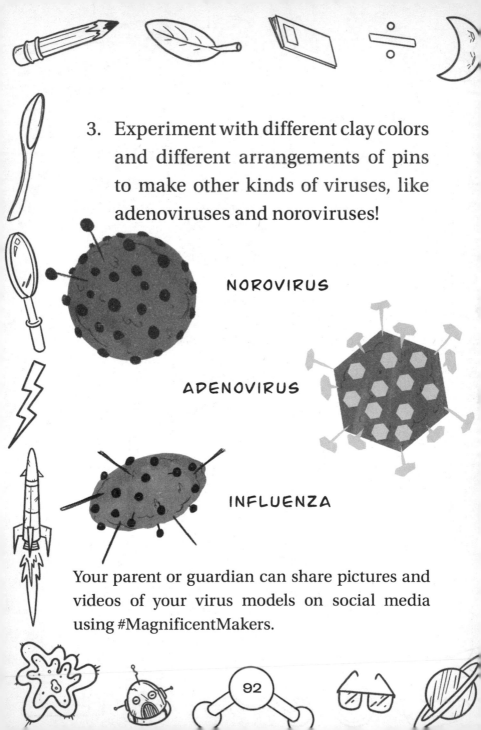

NOROVIRUS

ADENOVIRUS

INFLUENZA

Your parent or guardian can share pictures and videos of your virus models on social media using #MagnificentMakers.

≥MOLDY BREAD EXPERIMENT≤

MATERIALS

3 plastic sandwich bags
3 slices of bread
   clean fork
   clean towel or paper towel
   permanent marker
   soap and water

INSTRUCTIONS

1. Label each plastic bag as "untouched," "dirty hands," or "clean hands."

2. Remove one slice of bread from its bag with a clean fork. Place it in the plastic bag marked "untouched," and seal the bag.

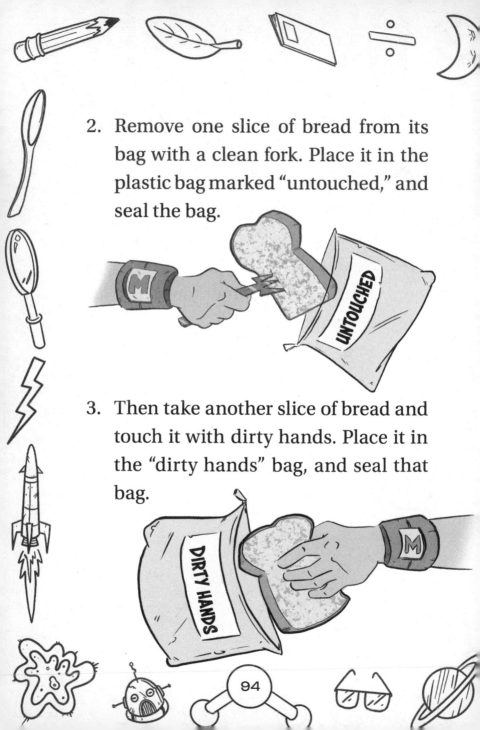

3. Then take another slice of bread and touch it with dirty hands. Place it in the "dirty hands" bag, and seal that bag.

4. Wash your hands for twenty seconds with soap and warm water. Dry them well with a clean towel or paper towel.

5. Take the final slice of bread and put it in the plastic bag labeled "clean hands." Seal the bag.

6. Store the bags on the counter-top or tape them to a wall for easy observation.
7. Observe the bags daily for one week. Which piece of bread has the most mold? Record your observations in a notebook or worksheet.*

*You can ask your parent or guardian to download a worksheet for this experiment at theannegriffith.com.

Get creative! You can also touch a slice of bread after using hand sanitizer, or rub bread slices on things around your house to find out what has the most germs!

Your parent or guardian can share pictures and videos of your moldy bread experiment on social media using #MagnificentMakers.

Missing the
Maker Maze already?

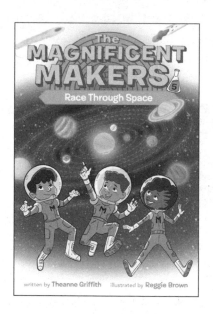

Read on for a peek at the
Magnificent Makers' next adventure!

"**M**agnificent Maker Watches ready?" shouted Dr. Crisp. She stood in front of the door with her hand on the knob.

"Yes!" replied the Makers, each holding an arm in the air. These special watches appeared on their wrists when they were about to start the challenge. They used them for all kinds of things in the Maker Maze, like shooting lasers, recording their answers, scanning holograms—and most importantly, keeping track of time.

"Good!" said Dr. Crisp. "We'll be traveling pretty far!"

The Makers needed to finish the challenge in less than one hundred twenty Maker Minutes if they wanted to return to the Maze for more fun. Dr. Crisp slowly opened the door, and the Makers' watches vibrated and glowed.

As Pablo, Violet, and Deepak walked through door number fourteen, their mouths dropped open. Rotating slowly in the middle of the wide room was a model solar system! In the center shone a bright yellow sun. Around it circled the eight different planets. And in between the orange glow of Mars and the stormy surface of Jupiter, tons of different-sized rocks floated like confetti.

Pablo pointed. "That must be the asteroid belt!" He definitely remembered reading about that. "It's the place in our solar system where most of the asteroids are found."

Violet reached out to run her fingertips through the edge of the model solar system.

BIZZAP!

"Okay, Makers. Listen up! For this level, we're going to get up close and personal with different space objects. But first, we'll need some special equipment!" Dr. Crisp pressed a button on the side of her watch and shouted, "Maker Maze, activate space suits!"

The room immediately went dark, and the floor began to vibrate. Suddenly, a blast of purple light shot out of the model sun and blinded the Makers.

BOOM! SNAP! WHIZ! ZAP!

After a few seconds, they were able to open their eyes again. The model solar system was gone. Pablo slowly lifted his arms to examine them. He patted his chest with his hands. Then he touched the helmet now covering his face.

"This is . . . ," Pablo began. But he couldn't find the word to finish his sentence.

"AMAZING!" Violet yelled as she jumped in the air.

The Makers were now wearing purple space suits! A black *M* was drawn on each of their chests. Clear helmets covered their faces. Dr. Crisp was in a space suit, too! Hers was black with a bright purple *M* on her chest. They all had silver space gloves.

"I can't believe it," said Deepak. "I'm a *real* astronaut!"

"You bet, space cadet!" said Dr. Crisp. "Okay, Makers. We need one last piece of equipment before we start." Dr. Crisp opened her backpack and began to pull out a long rope. She kept pulling . . . and pulling . . . and pulling. With one final tug, she said, "There! Now let's hook ourselves up."

"What is this for?" asked Violet. She looked closely at the four metal clasps attached to the rope.

"It looks like a leash," said Deepak.

"I know what it is!" said Pablo proudly. "It's a space tether!"

"What a *galactic* guess!" said Dr. Crisp. She gave Pablo a high five. "We're going to attach ourselves to this rope so that we all stay together. Wouldn't want anyone to get lost in space!" Dr. Crisp found the end of the very long rope. She tied it to a hook on the floor. Then she yelled into her watch, "Maker Maze, open *wormhole*!"

The ceiling slowly slid open. The Makers could only see blackness. Suddenly, a purple beam of light shot down from above.

"Cool!" said Violet.

"What is a wormhole?" asked Pablo. He started to walk in a circle around the glowing beam of light. "Is it like a portal?"

"No, a portal is more like a door," Deepak explained. "A wormhole is like a . . ." He thought for a moment. "A bridge! It connects places in space that are far apart."

"Well, shine my stars!" said Dr. Crisp. "You sure know your space stuff!"

Deepak smiled proudly. But Pablo felt a little bummed. Why didn't *he* know what a wormhole was? Didn't he read enough books at the library?

Dr. Crisp went around and hooked each Maker's suit to the rope. "Okay, Makers. No time to waste! Who's ready to race through space?" asked Dr. Crisp with a clap of her space gloves.

"We are!" the trio replied.

"Ready, set, BLAST OFF!"

Everyone jumped into the beam of light.

BIZZAP!

Acknowledgments

Thank you, Jorge, for being the most magnificent fan. I couldn't do this without your support. Dad, thank you for instilling your love of reading in me. I'm excited that we are both publishing books in 2021! Thank you, Mom, for being my guardian angel. I miss and love you always. To my daughters, Violeta and Lila, I love you both so much. You're a constant source of inspiration. My heart melts when you call a copy of the Magnificent Makers "Mommy's book." I do this for you both. Thank you, Caroline Abbey, for plucking me out of the Twitter-verse and giving me a chance. Finally, I'd like to thank my wonderful agent, Chelsea Eberly; my amazing editor, Tricia Lin; and the entire Random House team for your continued guidance and support.